For Flynn

Published 2017 by Walker Books Ltd, 87 Vauxhall Walk, London SE11 5HJ

This edition published 2018

1 3 5 7 9 10 8 6 4 2

Printed in China

British Library Cataloguing in Publication Data:
a catalogue record for this book is available from the British Library

ISBN 978-1-4063-8007-1

www.walker.co.uk
jezalborough.com

WALKER BOOKS
AND SUBSIDIARIES

LONDON • BOSTON • SYDNEY • AUCKLAND

PLAY

Jez Alborough

Mummy